MR. SILLY

by Roger Hargreaves

EGMONT

Mr Silly lives in Nonsenseland, which is a very funny place to live.

You see, in Nonsenseland, everything is as silly as can be.

In Nonsenseland the trees are pink!

And the grass is blue!

Isn't that silly?

In Nonsenseland dogs wear hats!

And do you know how birds fly in Nonsenseland?

No, they don't fly forwards.

They fly backwards!

It really is a very silly place indeed.

Which, of course, is why Mr Silly lives there.

Mr Silly, in fact, lives in quite the silliest-looking house you have ever seen in your whole life.

Have you ever seen a sillier-looking house than that?

Now, this particular story is all about the Nonsense Cup.

You see, in Nonsenseland each year they hold a competition, and the cup is awarded to whoever has the silliest idea of the year.

Mr Silly has never won the cup, but each night, lying in his bed, he dreamed about winning it.

In order to win the Nonsense Cup, Mr Silly realised that he would have to think up something remarkably silly.

He pondered over the problem one morning at breakfast.

Incidentally, you may be interested to know what Mr Silly was having for breakfast.

He was having a cup of coffee, which he put a spoonful of marmalade into.

After that he had a cornflake sandwich.

And to finish he had a boiled egg. But being Mr Silly, he ate the shell as well!

Isn't that a silly breakfast?

Anyway, this particular breakfast time, Mr Silly was thinking how to win that Cup.

He remembered two years ago the Cup was won by Mr Ridiculous.

He won by wallpapering his house.

Which sounds very ordinary, but in fact Mr Ridiculous had wallpapered the outside of his house!

And Mr Silly remembered last year when Mr Foolish won the Cup.

Mr Foolish, who was a friend of Mr Silly's, had won the Cup by inventing a car.

It was quite a normal car, apart from one thing. It had square wheels!

Isn't that silly?

Mr Silly thought and thought and thought, but it was no good.

He even had another cup of coffee with marmalade, but that didn't help either.

So he decided to take a walk.

Off he went, leaving his front door open so that he wouldn't have burglars when he was out.

On his walk, Mr Silly met a chicken wearing wellington boots and carrying an umbrella.

"Wouldn't it be silly if you didn't wear wellington boots and carry an umbrella?" he said to the chicken.

"Meow!" said the chicken, because animals in Nonsenseland don't make the same noises as they do in your country.

On his walk, Mr Silly met a worm wearing a top hat, a monocle and an old school tie.

"Wouldn't it be silly if you didn't wear a top hat, a monocle and an old school tie?" he said to the worm.

"Quack! Quack!" said the worm.

Next Mr Silly met a pig wearing trousers and a bowler hat.

"Wouldn't it be silly if you didn't wear trousers and a bowler hat?" he said to the pig.

"Moo!" said the pig.

Isn't that silly?

It was in the middle of Mr Silly's walk that he had his idea.

It was a beautifully silly idea.

Quite the silliest idea he'd ever had.

He hurried into town, and bought himself a pot of paint and a paintbrush.

PAI

The day of the great awarding of the Nonsense Cup arrived.

A huge crowd assembled in the City Square to see who was going to win the cup.

The King of Nonsenseland mounted the specially built platform.

"Ladies and gentlemen," he said to the crowd in the City Square. "It is my pleasure today to award the Nonsense Cup to whoever has had the silliest idea of the year."

"One of the silliest ideas of the year," continued the King, "is by Mr Muddle the farmer. He has managed to grow, of all things, a square apple!"

The crowd clapped as the square apple was held up by Mr Muddle for everybody to see.

He felt sure he was going to win.

“However,” said the King, and Mr Muddle’s face fell, “we have had an even sillier idea entered by Mrs Nincompoop.”

It was a teapot. Quite the silliest teapot there had ever been.

The crowd broke into thunderous applause.

“I therefore have great pleasure,” announced the King, “in presenting the Nonsense Cup to ...”

Just then he looked up, and stopped in astonishment.

Now, in the middle of the City Square there is a tree.

It's always been there, and it was at this tree that the King was looking in astonishment.

"What," he cried, "has happened to that tree?"

Everybody turned to look. The tree had green leaves!

Bright green leaves!

Not pink leaves like all the trees in Nonsenseland, but green.

There was an amazed silence.

"It was me," piped up Mr Silly. "I painted all the leaves green last night when you were all asleep!"

“A green tree!” exclaimed the King. “Whoever heard of a green tree?”

“A green tree!” shouted the crowd. “How silly!” And they started to applaud.

Mr Silly smiled modestly.

The King held up his hands.

“I think,” he said, “that this is the silliest idea I have ever heard of, and therefore I award the Nonsense Cup to Mr Silly!”

The crowd cheered and cheered.

Mr Silly went pink with pride.

And a bird, perched high up in the branches of the silly green tree, looked down.

"Woof!" it said, and flew off, backwards!